Fern and Her Not So Puffy Tail

SHANELL SAGER

AuthorHouse™
1663 Liberty Drive
Bloomington, IN 47403
www.authorhouse.com
Phone: 833-262-8899

This book is printed on acid-free paper.

ISBN: 978-1-6655-7924-7 (sc)
ISBN: 978-1-6655-7926-1 (hc)
ISBN: 978-1-6655-7925-4 (e)

Library of Congress Control Number: 2022923967

Print information available on the last page.

Published by AuthorHouse 01/12/2023

authorHOUSE

"For my daughter, may you always see the beauty in yourself and all things."

It was the first day of spring, and for Fern this was always the hardest day of the year. This was the day all the bunnies went outside and showed off their shiny spring tails. Fern did not have a big tail like the others, so the other bunnies would tease her and point out Fern's small fluff-less tail.

Fern looked in the mirror and wished for her tail to grow so they would not make fun of her anymore. That was when Fern's grand idea hopped into her mind. She was going to find herself a new cotton tail. Fern told her mom she was going for a walk and rushed out the door.

It felt like she had hopped for miles before she saw Red and Cisco's roadside stand.

"Howdy Fern, needing more carrots today?" whistled Red.

"No, not today fellas. I'm looking for a cotton tail."

"I've got just the thing for you!" said Cisco

Fern took a big whiff, "PHEW! I can't walk around smelling like that!"

Red spoke up. "I've got another idea."

Red got out his bailing twine and handed it to Fern to tie on a piece of cauliflower. "What do you think of it?" he asked.

"It's beautiful, but is it going to hold?" Fern wiggled to test it out, and her cauliflower tail fell to her knees.

"Maybe you could try the new store in town."

"Great idea, Red!"

Fern waved goodbye and hopped off to the shop.

"Hello, I'm Hashtag. How may I help you today?"

"I'm looking for a new cotton tail."

"Okay, let's look in the tank decor."

Hashtag looked back at Fern.

"Hello, my name is Hashtag. Can I help you find anything?"

"I am going to try on some tank decor." Fern giggled.

"Oh yes, that's on aisle three."

Fern found a plastic sea urchin, but it was TOO big.

Beside it on the shelf was some fake coral. Fern held it up to her tail.

"OUCH! It scratched me."

"Oh no. You should go to the pharmacy down the street."

"Thank you!"

"Hello, may I interest you in our new bunny treats?"

"No thanks," giggled Fern.

The gloomy clouds matched Fern's disappointment.

"Hello Fern," said Spice. "You look like you need some cream for that."

Spice handed Fern a cotton ball. While putting on the medicine, the cotton ball stuck to Fern's scratch and left a fluffy tail clinging on.

Fern jumped with glee, but her celebration didn't last very long.

CRACKLE-BOOM!

"Oh no! My new tail!"

Fern ran for cover, but it was too late. Her puffy cotton ball had turned to a squelchy mush.

Three hairdressers spotted Fern and asked her what was wrong.

"I don't have a fuzzy cotton tail like all the other rabbits. I only have this tiny thing."

"Well," said the first one, "we will see what we can do."

"That is so sweet of you, but I don't think there is anything that can fix it."

"Honey, look at my hair. I do NOT wake up looking like this. We could dye your tail to give it color."

"Or-I-could-give-it-a-perm," the second one said energetically.

"And I could give it as much volume as I can," added the third.

Fern sniffled. "Okay, let's give it a try."

"We-are-almost-finished! I-can't-wait-for-you-to-see-how-it-looks," jabbered the second one.

SCRUNCH, SWISH, PSHHHH!

"What do you think?" the first one asked.

"I suppose it's fluffier than it was before," said Fern.

"Just remember, you're a beautiful bunny no matter what your tail looks like!"

"Thank you again ladies, I appreciate your help," said Fern.

Fern walked towards home, thinking about everything that had happened.

All the people she met had made her feel so much better. Then BAM! Fern finally understood, and she took off like lightning to head back home.

Passing the roadside stand she stopped and told Red and Cisco of her inspiring day.

"Wow! What a day," whinnied Red.

"On top of it all, I see how truly exceptional my friends are. The hairdressers make everyone look and feel their best, Spice made my scratch stop hurting, Hashtag was a thoughtful store owner, and you both have hearts of gold. Well bye fellas, I've got to get home!"

Fern looked in the mirror for the second time that day, and she saw exactly what she needed to see.

Fern smiled as she thought to herself, "I am ready to show off MY cotton tail."

Psalm 139:14(NKJV)

"I will praise You, for I am fearfully and wonderfully made."

CPSIA information can be obtained
at www.ICGtesting.com
Printed in the USA
LVHW071947180223
739854LV00007B/41

9 781665 579247